Treasury of Illustrated Classics™

Alice in Wonderland

by
Lewis Carroll

Adapted by
Susan Linney

Illustrated by
Rex Schneider

Modern Publishing
A Division of Unisystems, Inc.
New York, New York 10022

Series UPC: 39340

Cover art by Michele Nidenoff

Contents

Chapter 1

Down the Rabbit Hole

Alice was beginning to get very tired of sitting next to her sister on the riverbank with nothing to do. Once or twice she looked at the book her sister was reading, but it had no pictures or conversations in it. "What is the use of a book," thought Alice, "without pictures or conversations?"

All of a sudden, a White Rabbit with pink eyes dashed across the countryside. "Oh, dear!" the Rabbit exclaimed. "I'm late, late, late!" Alice thought such a

sight was peculiar, and she was especially surprised when the Rabbit took a watch out of his waistcoat pocket and checked the time. Burning with curiosity, Alice ran after the animal and was just in time to see it pop down a large rabbit hole.

In another moment Alice went down after it, without considering how she might get back up. The hole dipped suddenly and Alice found herself falling down what seemed to be a very deep well. Down, down, down she fell. Either the well was very deep, or Alice fell very slowly, because she had plenty of time to look around her and wonder what was going to happen next.

As she slowly floated downward, Alice noticed that the walls on either side were lined with cupboards and bookshelves. She grabbed a jar from one of the shelves as she moved past it. It was labeled ORANGE MARMALADE but, to her great disappointment, it was empty. Alice did not want to drop the jar, for fear that she might hit someone underneath, so she put it into one of the cupboards as she floated by.

"Well," thought Alice, "after a fall like this, I shall think nothing of falling down stairs. How very brave they will think me at home!"

Down, down, down she fell. Would the fall *never* come to an end? "I must be getting toward the center of the world," Alice thought. "How funny it will seem to come out on the other side and be among people who walk upside down."

Down, down, down she went. There was nothing for Alice to do but wait. "My cat Dinah will miss me very much tonight," she remarked. "I hope they'll remember to give her milk and feed her. Oh, Dinah, I wish you were down here with me. There are no mice in the air for you to catch, but you might catch a bat and that's very much like a mouse, you know. But do cats eat bats, I wonder? Do cats eat bats?"

As Alice pondered this question, she dozed off while still floating slowly down the hole. Suddenly, thump! thump!—she landed on a heap of dry leaves and the fall was over.

chapter 2
The Golden Key

Alice was not a bit hurt. She jumped up and looked around her. She caught sight of the White Rabbit, hurrying down a long passage, all the while exclaiming to himself, "Oh, my ears and whiskers, how it's getting late!" Alice ran after the odd creature, which turned a corner and disappeared. Alice found herself in a long, low hall lit by a row of lamps hanging from the roof.

There were doors all around the hall. Alice tried to open each one, but all were locked. After she had been all the way down one side of the hall and up the other, trying every door a second time, she walked sadly down the middle, wondering how she would ever get herself out of this mess.

Her thoughts were interrupted when she noticed a three-legged table, made of glass, just ahead of her. A tiny golden key lay upon it. Alice thought that she had found the way to unlock one of the doors, but she was wrong. Either the

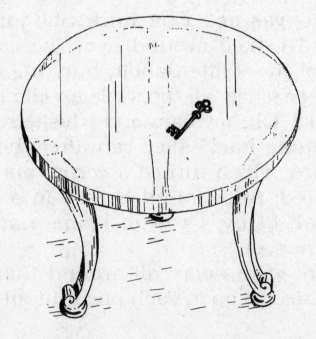

locks were too large or the key was too small, because the key would not open any of the doors. Alice was about to give up when she noticed a plush, red curtain in the corner of the hallway. Behind it was a tiny door, about 15 inches high. Alice put the little golden key in the lock and, to her great delight, it fit!

She opened the tiny door, knelt down, peered in, and discovered the most beautiful garden she had ever seen. "I'd love to be in there," she thought. "This hallway is dark and empty, but that garden is absolutely gorgeous!"

Unfortunately, the door was so small that Alice could not get even her head through it. "Even if my head would go through," she thought, "it would be of very little use because my shoulders wouldn't. Oh, I wish I could fit through this door! I think I could, if I only knew how to begin." Things had been so peculiar so far that, at this point, Alice thought almost anything was possible.

There was no use in waiting near the door, so Alice went back to the glass table. Sitting on it was a tiny bottle with a label tied to it that read DRINK ME. "*This* certainly was not here before," Alice said aloud. Being a very smart girl, she was not about to follow the tag's instructions without thinking it over carefully first.

Putting the key down on the table, she thought, "I'll examine the bottle, and see whether it's marked POISON." Alice had heard stories of children who had gotten into trouble because they had not followed the simple rules their parents had taught them. One thing she had always been told was that if you drank from a bottle marked POISON, it is almost certain to disagree with you sooner or later.

This bottle was not marked POISON, so Alice decided to try it. The flavor was an odd mixture of cherry tart, custard, pineapple, roast turkey, toffee, and hot buttered toast. She finished it off anyway—and suddenly she began to feel very strange.

"What a curious feeling," she said. "I must be shrinking!"

So it was! She was now only 10 inches high—the perfect size to fit through the door and wander into the beautiful garden! Alice waited to see if she would shrink more, frightened by the idea of getting any smaller than she already was.

"What if I keep getting smaller and smaller," she worried, "until there is nothing left of me? I wonder what I would be like then!"

When nothing happened for a few minutes, Alice decided to go into the garden. But when she got to the door, poor Alice realized that she had forgotten the little golden key! She could see it high above, on top of the glass table. Now that she was only 10 inches high, she could not possibly reach it. She tried to climb up one of the table legs, but it was too slippery. After she had tired herself out, a sad and frustrated Alice sat down and cried.

She sobbed for some time, until her eyes fell on a little box lying under the table. Alice dried her eyes, opened the box, and found a small cake inside with the words EAT ME on it. "I'll eat it," Alice said. "After all, if it makes me grow larger, I'll be able to reach the key. If it makes me grow smaller, I'll be able to

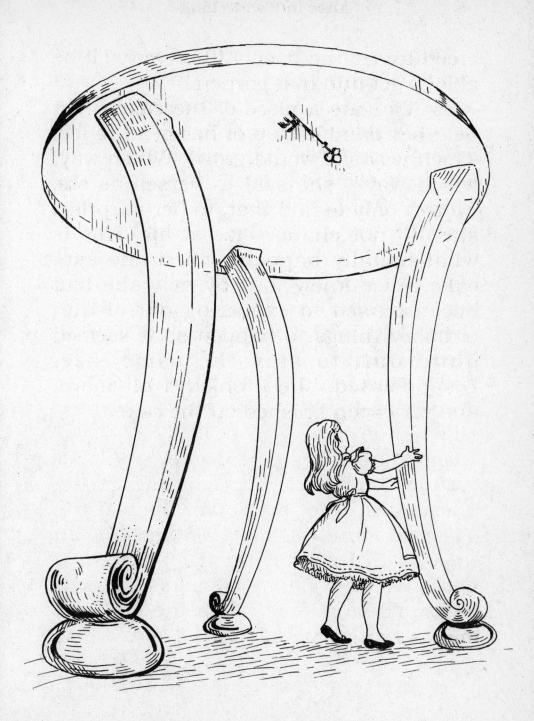

creep under the door. Either way, I'll be able to get into that garden."

So Alice ate a piece of the cake, then held her hand on top of her head to feel which way she would grow. "Which way, which way?" she said to herself as she waited, only to find that, to her surprise, she did not change size at all. This is what usually happens when one eats cake, Alice knew, but by now she had become used to expecting out-of-the-ordinary things to happen so it seemed quite dull to stay the same size. Disappointed, she nibbled a bit more, and very soon finished off the cake.

chapter 3

How Alice Grew Tall

"Curiouser and curiouser," thought Alice, when she realized that she *was* in fact changing in some way. "Now I'm shooting up like a telescope—the largest that ever was! Good-bye, feet," she cried, for when she looked down, they seemed to be almost completely out of sight. "Oh, my poor little feet, I wonder who will put on your shoes and stockings? I'm sure I won't be able! I'll be too far off to trouble myself about you, so you must manage

the best way you can. But I must be kind to them," she thought, "or perhaps they won't walk the way I want them to go!"

Just that moment, Alice's head hit the roof of the hall. She was now more than nine feet high—tall enough to reach the golden key! She grabbed it and hurried to open the garden door. But poor Alice was now so big that she could barely even peer through the tiny door. She had to lie down on one side and look into the garden with one eye. To get through was more hopeless than ever. Alice put the key back on the table and began to cry again.

"You ought to be ashamed of yourself," Alice muttered to herself through her tears. "A big girl like you, crying this way." But she kept on sobbing, shedding gallons of tears, until there was a large pool around her, about four inches deep and reaching halfway down the hall.

After a time, Alice heard the pattering of little feet in the distance. She dried her eyes to see what was coming. It was the

White Rabbit, splendidly dressed, with a pair of white gloves in one hand and a large fan in the other. He was trotting along in a great hurry, muttering to himself, "Oh, the Duchess, the Duchess! Oh, she'll be angry if I've kept her waiting!"

Alice felt relieved to see someone who might be able to help her. When the Rabbit came near she timidly began, "If you please, sir—" The Rabbit was so startled by the sound of her voice—and the size of her body—that he dropped the gloves and fan and scurried off. He was gone once again.

Alice picked up the gloves and fan and began fanning herself. (The hall was quite hot.) "Oh, dear," she thought, "how odd everything is today! Yesterday, everything went on just as usual. I wonder if I changed during the night? Was I the same when I got up this morning? I think I can remember feeling a little different. But if I'm not the same girl, who in the world *am* I?" She began thinking

about all the children she knew who were the same age, wondering if she could have changed into any of them.

"I can't be Ada," Alice said, "for her hair has such long ringlets and mine doesn't have any ringlets at all. I can't be Mabel," she continued, "for she has trouble with her times tables and I know them all by heart! Besides, she is *she* and I am *I*—oh, how puzzling it all is!"

Alice thought some more. "I wonder if I know all the things that I used to know. Let me see . . . London is the capital of Paris, and Paris is the capital of Rome, and Rome—no, no, that's all wrong! Let's try the multiplication tables. Four times five is twelve," she recited, "and four times six is thirteen, and four times seven is—oh dear, that's all wrong, too! I *must* have been changed into Mabel during the night, and if I'm Mabel, I'll have to go live in *her* house and play with *her* toys, and I'll have so many lessons to learn!"

"No!" Alice said sharply to herself. "If I'm Mabel, I'll stay down here! It'll be no use for people to put their heads down and say, 'Come up again, dear!' I'll just look up and say, 'Who am I, then? Tell me that first and then, if I like being that person, I'll come up. If not, I'll stay down here until I'm somebody else!' But oh dear," Alice continued as she burst into tears once more, "I do wish *some-one* would look down and find me! I'm so tired of being all alone down here!"

As Alice said this, she looked down at her hands and was surprised to find that one of the Rabbit's tiny white gloves was on one of them. It fit her perfectly.

"How could that be?" she wondered. "I must be growing small again!" She got up and went to the glass table to measure herself. Alice found that she now was about two feet high and shrinking rapidly. Suddenly, she realized that the fan she was holding was making her shrink. She dropped it just in time to save herself from shrinking away completely.

"That was a narrow escape!" Alice said. "Now, for the garden!" She ran back to the little door, but alas! It was shut again, and locked, and the little golden key was lying high above on the glass table as before. "Things are more mixed up than ever!" poor Alice exclaimed.

But they were about to get even worse. All of a sudden, Alice's tiny foot slipped on something. Splash! She was up to her chin in salt water.

Chapter 4
The Pool of Tears

At first Alice thought that she had somehow fallen into the sea, but she soon realized that she was swimming in the pool of tears she had wept when she was nine feet tall.

"I wish I hadn't cried so much!" she said as she swam about, trying to find dry land. "I'll be punished for it now, I suppose, by drowning in my own tears!"

Just then Alice heard something splashing, so she swam over to find out what it was. It was a mouse that had slipped into the big pool, just like she had done.

"Would it be of any use," she thought, "if I spoke with this mouse? Everything is so strange down here, it's very likely that the creature can talk. There is no harm in trying, I guess." So Alice called, "Oh, Mouse!"

The Mouse looked at her with wonder and seemed to wink one of its little eyes, but said nothing.

"Perhaps it doesn't understand English," thought Alice. "Maybe it's a French mouse." So she began: "*Oú est ma chatte?*" That was the first sentence of her French book; it meant, "Where is my cat?" At this, the Mouse leaped up and began to look around, shaking with fright.

"Oh, I beg your pardon," Alice said quickly. "I forgot that you don't like cats!"

"Not like cats!" the Mouse cried sharply. "Would *you* like cats if you were me?"

"I suppose not," said Alice. "Please don't be angry. Though I wish I could introduce you to my cat, Dinah. I think you would change your mind about cats

if you met her. She's such a dear, quiet
thing," Alice went on dreamily, while
swimming about in the pool. "She sits
calmly by the fire, licking her paws and
washing her face. She's so soft to pet,

and she's so good at catching mice—" At this, the Mouse began to shake again.

"Oh, I beg your pardon!" Alice cried. "We won't talk about Dinah any more."

"Please!" cried the Mouse, still trembling with fear. "Don't let me hear her name again!"

"Okay, I promise," Alice said, and changed the subject. "Do you like dogs? There is a nice, little dog I know that I'd like you to see. A little, bright-eyed terrier, with long, curly, brown hair! It fetches things when you throw them. It will also sit up and beg for its dinner, and all sorts of other things. It belongs to a farmer, and he says that it's so useful because it kills all the rats, and—oh dear!" cried Alice. "I'm afraid I've upset the poor thing again!" Indeed she had; the Mouse was paddling furiously away from her, making quite a commotion in the pool as it went.

Alice called softly after it, "Mouse, dear, do come back again! I'm so sorry I

frightened you! I promise I won't talk about cats or dogs, if you don't like them!" The Mouse turned around and swam slowly back to her.

"Let's get back to shore," it said to Alice. So, together, they swam back to the edge of the pool.

chapter 5
The White Rabbit's House

Once they reached the shore, they shook themselves off. The Mouse took one more look at Alice, then it scurried off.

"How rude!" Alice thought, but soon forgot about it, for the White Rabbit suddenly appeared again, this time muttering to himself, "The Duchess! Oh, my dear paws! Oh, my fur and whiskers! She'll have me executed! Where could I have put them?"

Alice guessed in a moment that he was looking for the fan and white gloves. She looked around but could not find them anywhere. Everything seemed to have changed since her swim in the pool. The long hall, glass table, and little door had vanished. She was now in what seemed to be a heavily wooded forest.

The Rabbit soon noticed Alice hunting for the gloves and fan. "Mary Anne," he called to her, in an angry tone. "What are you doing here? Run home this instant and fetch me a pair of gloves and a fan!" Alice was so startled by the Rabbit's tone that she took off at once, without trying to explain that she was, in fact, *not* Mary Anne.

"He must have taken me for his housemaid," Alice supposed. "How surprised he'll be when he finds out who I really am! But I'd better go get him the gloves and fan—if I can find them."

As Alice said this, she came upon a neat little house. On the door was a

bright brass plate with the name W. Rabbit engraved on it. She went in without knocking and hurried up the stairs.

"How odd this is," Alice said as she hunted around. "Running errands for a rabbit! I suppose Dinah will be sending me on errands next!" Alice imagined her cat ordering her about.

"Alice, come here at once," Dinah would say. "Watch this mouse hole for me and make sure the mouse doesn't get out!"

"Only I don't think," Alice went on, "that my parents would let Dinah in the house if she began ordering people around like that!"

By this time, Alice had found her way into a tidy little room with a table next to the window, and on that table was a fan and several pairs of white gloves. Alice picked them up and was about to leave the room when she noticed a little bottle sitting by the mirror. This bottle had no label that read DRINK ME, but nonetheless Alice popped the cork and put it to her lips.

"Something interesting always happens whenever I eat or drink anything here," she thought. "So I'll see what this bottle does. I hope it makes me grow large again, for I'm tired of being so tiny!"

It did so, indeed, and much sooner than Alice had expected. Before she had drunk even half the bottle, she felt her

head pressing against the ceiling, and she had to bend down to keep her neck from being broken. She put down the bottle, saying, "That's quite enough, thank you. I don't want to grow anymore. I wish I hadn't swallowed so much!"

It was too late for such a wish, though. Alice kept growing and growing, and soon

she had to kneel down on the floor. In another minute, there was not even room for this, so she had to lie down with one elbow against the door and the other arm curled around her head. Still, she grew! Finally, she had to put one arm out the window and one foot up the chimney. "I can do no more," she thought to herself. "What will become of me?"

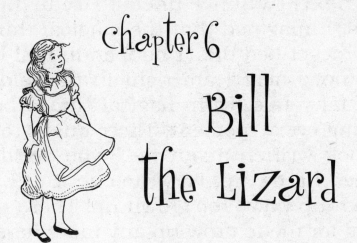

chapter 6
Bill
the Lizard

Luckily for Alice, she did not grow any bigger. Still, she was extremely uncomfortable and there seemed no way for her to get out of the house.

"It was much more pleasant at home," thought Alice, "where one wasn't always growing smaller or bigger, or being ordered around by mice and rabbits. I almost wish I had never gone down that rabbit hole. Yet, this sort of life is quite exciting. I wonder what will happen to me next? When I used to read fairy tales, I imagined that the magical things they described didn't happen in real life. But now, here I am right in the middle of a fairy tale, with magical things happening every moment! There ought to be a book written about me," she decided. "When I grow up, I'll write one. But I *am* grown up now. *Too* grown up! There's no room for me to grow up any more here."

Alice continued talking to herself, going over all the odd things about her experience so far, until she heard a voice outside the house and stopped to listen.

"Mary Anne! Mary Anne!" said the voice. "Fetch me my gloves this instant!"

Alice then heard a pattering of feet on the stairs, and realized that it was the White Rabbit coming to look for her.

Afraid of being scolded, Alice trembled, shaking the house, quite forgetting that she was about a thousand times larger than the Rabbit and had no reason to be afraid of him.

The White Rabbit came up to the door and tried to open it. The door opened inward, however, and Alice's elbow was pressed hard against it, so he couldn't get in. "I'll go around and get in at the window," Alice heard him remark.

"No, you won't," thought Alice, annoyed, realizing that she need not be bossed around by a rabbit that was not even half her size. She waited until she heard him at the window, then suddenly spread out her hand and tried to catch hold of the little thing. She did not grab anything, but heard a shriek and a crash of breaking glass. She thought she must have caused the Rabbit to fall.

"Pat! Pat!" Alice heard the angry Rabbit exclaim. "Where are you?"

"Right here," answered a voice that Alice had not heard before. "I'm digging for apples, Your Honor."

"Digging for apples, indeed!" snapped the Rabbit. "Come help me out of here at once." At this, Alice heard more sounds

of breaking glass, then the Rabbit said, "Now tell me, Pat, what's in that window?"

"It appears to be an arm, Your Honor," replied the voice.

"An arm!" exclaimed the Rabbit. "Whoever saw one that size? It fills the whole window!"

"That it does, Your Honor," replied Pat in a matter-of-fact tone, "but it's an arm, nonetheless. I'm sure of it."

"Well, it's got no business here," replied the Rabbit. "Go and take it away at once!"

There was a long silence after this. Alice listened very closely, but she could hear only whispers by the window. She spread out her hand and made another grab in the air. This time, she heard two little shrieks and even more sounds of breaking glass.

"I wonder what they'll do next?" Alice thought. "As for taking me away, I wish they could. I don't want to stay here any longer!"

Alice waited for a while without hearing anything. Finally, she noticed a rumbling noise, followed by the sound of many voices talking together. Alice was able to make out: "Where's the other ladder? I only have one. Bill's got the other. Bill, put it over here!" The strange voices were making some kind of plan to get the giant Alice out of the little house.

"Bill, Bill!" one of the voices cried. "You've got to go down the chimney!"

"So Bill has to come down the chimney, has he?" Alice thought. "Poor Bill seems to have to do everything. Well, this fireplace seems narrow enough, but I think I can kick a little."

Alice pulled her foot down the chimney as far as she could, and waited until she heard a little animal—she couldn't guess what sort it was—scratching about, trying to climb down. She gave one sharp kick, then waited to see what would happen next.

The first thing she heard was a chorus

of voices outside exclaiming, "There goes Bill!" Next, she heard the Rabbit's voice, calling, "Catch him!"

After a short silence, then a loud thump, Alice heard the whole collection of voices saying, "Hold up his head!— How was it, old fellow?—Are you all right?—Tell us about it, Bill!"

At last came a feeble, squeaky voice, which Alice assumed to be Bill's. "Well, I hardly know," he said. "I'm a bit too flustered to talk about it. All I know is, something came at me like a jack-in-the-box and up I went like a sky-rocket!"

"So you did, old fellow," said the voices in unison.

"We must burn down the house!" Alice heard the White Rabbit say.

At that, Alice called out, as loud as she could, "If you do, I'll set Dinah the cat on you!" There was a dead silence. "I wonder what they'll do now?" Alice thought. "If they had any sense, they'd take the roof off."

Instead, the group began to throw little pebbles through the window, some of which hit Alice's face. "I'll put a stop to this," she thought, but then she noticed that the pebbles were turning into little cakes! "If I eat one of them," she thought, "it's sure to change my size in

some way. I can't grow any larger, so it will have to make me smaller."

She swallowed one of the cakes and was delighted to find herself shrinking right away. As soon as she was small enough, Alice ran out of the house and found a crowd of little birds and other animals waiting outside. Poor Bill—who, it turns out, is a lizard—was in the middle of the crowd, being held up by his friends. The crowd rushed at Alice the minute she appeared, but she ran as fast as she could and managed to escape into a thickly wooded area.

"The first thing I have to do," Alice decided, "is to grow to my proper size again. Once I've done that, I have to find my way into that lovely garden. I think that will be the best plan."

It was an excellent plan, indeed, but she didn't have the slightest idea how to go about it. "Perhaps I'll find another cake," she hoped, "that will make me grow to my real size."

Alice was sitting next to a tree, trying to figure things out, when she noticed a large mushroom growing nearby. It was about the same height as she was now, and after looking under it and on both sides, she decided to see if there was anything on top of it.

She stretched up on tiptoe and peered over the edge of the mushroom. Her eyes immediately met those of a large, blue caterpillar that was sitting on top of the mushroom with folded arms, quietly smoking a hookah pipe. How odd, indeed, this seemed to Alice.

chapter 7
Advice from a Caterpillar

Alice and the Caterpillar stared at each other for some time in silence. At last, the Caterpillar took the pipe out of its mouth and addressed her in a lazy, sleepy voice.

"Who are *you*?" the odd-looking, blue creature asked.

This was not an encouraging conversation opener, but Alice replied, "I—I hardly know, sir. I know who I was when

I got up this morning, but I must have changed several times since then."

"What do you mean by that?" the Caterpillar asked sternly. "Explain yourself at once!"

"I *can't* explain myself," Alice replied, "because I'm not myself, you see."

"I don't see," said the Caterpillar.

"I'm afraid I can't put it more clearly," Alice went on, "for I can't understand myself. Being so many different sizes in one day is very confusing."

"It is not," said the Caterpillar.

"Well, perhaps *you* haven't found it so yet," Alice snapped back, "but one day you will turn into a butterfly and then you'll feel odd, won't you?"

"Not a bit," the Caterpillar answered.

"Well, perhaps *your* feelings are different," said Alice. "All I know is, it would feel very odd to me."

"You!" said the Caterpillar angrily. "Who are *you*?"

This brought them back to the very

beginning. Alice was getting fed up with the insect's remarks, so she said, "I think you ought to tell me who *you* are, first."

"Why?" the Caterpillar asked.

Alice did not know quite how to answer that. As she did not have a good reply, she gave up and began to walk away.

"Wait!" said the Caterpillar. "Come back! I have something important to say."

Alice turned around and listened.

"Keep your temper," it said.

"Is that all?" said Alice, annoyed.

"No," said the Caterpillar. It paused a few moments before continuing. "So you think you're changed, do you?"

"I'm afraid I am, sir," Alice said. "I can't remember things as I used to, and I don't stay the same size for more than ten minutes at a time!"

"What size do you want to be?"

"Oh, I'm not particular," Alice said. "I just don't like changing so often, you see."

"I *don't* see," the Caterpillar said rudely. "Are you content now?"

"Well, I would like to be a little larger, sir, if you wouldn't mind," Alice replied. "Three inches is a terrible height to be!"

"It is a very *good* height," the Caterpillar said, offended, pulling itself upright. (It was exactly three inches tall.)

"For *you*, perhaps," Alice replied, "but I'm not used to it!"

"You'll get used to it in time," said the Caterpillar.

Alice was tired of going back and forth with this creature, so she decided to

wait until it chose to speak again. After a minute or two, the Caterpillar yawned lazily. As it climbed down off the mushroom and crawled away into the grass, it said, "One side will make you grow taller and the other side will make you grow shorter."

"One side of *what?*" Alice thought to herself. "The other side of *what?*"

"Of the mushroom," said the Caterpillar, as if it had read her mind. In another moment, the creature slinked off and was soon out of sight.

chapter 8

A Pesky Pigeon

Alice looked thoughtfully at the mushroom for a moment, trying to make out its two sides. It was perfectly round, so Alice found this difficult to do. At last, she stretched her arms around the mushroom as far as they would go, then broke off a bit of the edge with each hand.

"Now which is which?" Alice whispered to herself. She nibbled a little of the right-hand piece to see what would happen. At

once, she felt a violent blow underneath her chin, which had struck her foot!

Alice was frightened by her sudden, dramatic shrinking, but knowing that there was no time to be lost, she quickly chewed on some of the left-hand piece of mushroom, hoping it would reverse the effect.

It did, and Alice was relieved when she started growing—until she realized that her shoulders were nowhere to be seen. All Alice could see, as she looked down, was an extremely long neck that seemed to rise like a stalk out of a sea of green leaves far below.

"What is all that green stuff?" said Alice, "and where have my shoulders gone? Oh, and my poor hands! Why can't I see you?" Alice was sure that she was moving them as she spoke, but no result seemed to follow, except a little shaking among the distant leaves.

There seemed to be no chance of getting her hands to reach her head, so

Alice tried moving her head down to her hands. She was delighted to find that her neck bent easily in almost any direction, just like a snake. So she started to dive down into the greenery, which she found to be the tops of the trees under which she had been wandering. Then a sharp hiss made her pull back in a hurry. A large pigeon had flown into Alice's face and was hitting her hard with its wings.

"Serpent!" screamed the Pigeon. "Serpent!"

"I am not a serpent," Alice exclaimed. "Leave me alone!"

"Serpent, I say!" repeated the Pigeon. "There's no way of pleasing you!"

"I haven't the slightest idea what you're talking about," Alice replied.

"I've tried the roots of trees, and I've tried riverbanks, and I've tried hedges," the Pigeon explained. "But those serpents! There's no pleasing them!"

Alice was more and more puzzled, but

knew that there was no use in saying more until the Pigeon had finished.

"As if it wasn't trouble enough hatching the eggs," the Pigeon continued, "I have to be on the lookout for serpents day and night! I haven't had a wink of sleep in three weeks!"

"I'm very sorry that you've been bothered," Alice said kindly. She now under-

stood that the Pigeon thought she was after its eggs.

"Just as I thought I'd found the highest tree in the woods, far from any snake," said the Pigeon, "you swoop down from the sky!"

"But I'm not a serpent," Alice pleaded. "I'm a— I'm a—"

"Well," the Pigeon demanded, "what are you, then?"

"I'm a little girl," said Alice, rather doubtfully, as she thought of all the changes she had gone through today.

The Pigeon laughed. "A likely story, indeed! I've seen many little girls in my time, but never one with a neck like yours! No, no, you're a serpent, and there's no use denying it. I suppose you'll be telling me next that you've never eaten an egg."

"I have eaten eggs, certainly," said Alice, "but little girls eat eggs just as serpents do!"

"I don't believe it," snapped the

Pigeon. "If they do, then they're a kind of serpent, that's all I can say."

This was a new idea to Alice, so she was silent for a moment while she thought it over. Then the Pigeon added, "You're looking for eggs, so what does it matter to me whether you're a little girl or a serpent?"

"It matters a good deal to *me*," Alice replied. "I am not looking for eggs. If I was, I wouldn't want *yours*—I don't like them raw!"

"Well, be off, then," the Pigeon said as it settled back down into its nest. Alice crouched down among the trees as best she could. Her neck kept getting caught in the branches, and every now and then she had to stop to free it. When she finally found her hands, she realized that she was still clutching the two pieces of the mushroom, so she set to work very carefully, nibbling first at one and then at the other. With each bite, she grew a little taller, then a little shorter, until she was back to her normal height.

It had been a while since she was her normal size, so it felt strange at first. But Alice got used to it after a few moments and began talking to herself, as usual.

"Half my plan already accomplished!" she thought proudly. "I'm back to my regular size. The next thing is to find a way into that garden. How, I wonder?"

As she said this, Alice came upon a tiny house that was no taller than her knee. "Whoever lives there," she thought, "would be awfully afraid of me at this height! I would frighten them out of their wits!" So Alice nibbled more of the mushroom until she had brought herself down to nine inches.

chapter 9

Pig and Pepper

For a minute or two Alice stood outside the house, hesitant to go inside. Suddenly, a footman came running out of the woods. The footman was a fish, but Alice had gotten so used to this odd world that she barely even blinked at the sight.

The Fish-footman rapped at the door. Alice watched as it was opened by another footman—a frog with large, round eyes.

"For the Duchess," the Fish said, as he

handed over a large letter. "It's an invitation from the Queen to play croquet."

"From the Queen," said the Frog in the
same tone. "An invitation for the Duchess
to play croquet."

At this, the Fish-footman left, leaving
the Frog-footman alone by the closed
door, holding the oversized envelope and
staring stupidly into the sky. Alice walked
past him and knocked on the door.

"There's no use in knocking," the
Frog-footman said, "for two reasons.

First, because I am on the same side of the door you are, so I can't let you in. Second, because they are making so much noise inside, no one could possibly hear you."

Indeed, there was quite a racket coming from inside the house. A constant howling and sneezing sound could be heard, followed every now and then by a loud crash, as if a dish or kettle had been broken to pieces.

"Please, then," Alice said. "How am I to get in?"

"There might be some sense in your knocking," the Frog-footman continued, ignoring her question, "if we had the door between us. If you were inside, for instance, you might knock and then I'd let you out. Or if you were outside and I was in, I might let you in."

"How am I to get in?" Alice repeated.

Still ignoring her, the Frog-footman continued to stare into the sky. "I shall sit here," he said, "'til tomorrow—"

At this moment, the door of the house opened and a large plate flew out, aimed at the Frog-footman's head. It grazed his nose, then shattered against one of the trees behind him. Then the door slammed shut.

"—or the next day, maybe," the Frog-footman went on, as if nothing unusual had happened.

"How am I to get in?" Alice asked yet again, although she wasn't sure she wanted to enter a house in which plates were flying about.

"Are you to get in at all?" said the Frog-footman. "That is the question, you know."

Alice did know, but she didn't like to be told so. "It's really dreadful," Alice thought to herself, "how these creatures argue all the time. It's enough to drive a person crazy!" Then she said to the Frog-footman, "What am I to do?"

"Anything you'd like," he replied, then he began whistling.

"Oh, there's no use in talking to him," Alice muttered to herself. She opened the door and went in.

She found herself in a large kitchen that was full of smoke. The Duchess sat on a stool in the center of the room, nursing a baby. A cook was leaning over the fire, stirring a large cauldron that seemed to be full of soup.

"There's too much pepper in that soup!" Alice said to herself as she let out a big sneeze. There seemed to be too much pepper in the air, too. Even the Duchess sneezed occasionally, and the poor baby was sneezing and howling without a moment's pause. The only two creatures in the room not sneezing were the cook and a large cat that was lying on the floor, grinning from ear to ear.

"Would you tell me, please," Alice asked politely, "why your cat grins like that?"

"It's a Cheshire cat, that's why," said the Duchess, not at all surprised by Alice's presence.

"I didn't know that Cheshire cats grinned," Alice replied. "In fact, I didn't know that cats *could* grin."

"They all can," the Duchess said, "and most of 'em do."

"I don't know of *any* that do," Alice said politely.

"You don't know much," the Duchess said, "and that's a fact."

Alice was hurt by the rudeness of the Duchess's remark. She was about to change the subject when the cook suddenly started throwing everything within her reach across the room. Fire-irons, saucepans, plates, and dishes all went flying through the air, occasionally hitting the Duchess, but more often hitting the wall. The baby kept howling nonstop, but the Duchess didn't seem to notice the chaos.

"Oh, *please* watch what you're doing!" Alice pleaded, concerned for the baby's well-being. To her relief, the cook stopped throwing things and went back to stirring the soup.

"If everybody minded their own business," the Duchess said, "the world would go around much faster than it does."

"Which would not be an advantage," said Alice, who was glad for the chance to show off what she had learned in school. "You see, Earth takes twenty-four hours to turn on its axis—"

"Speaking of axes," the Duchess interrupted, "off with her head!"

Alice glanced anxiously at the cook to see whether she would obey the Duchess's order. Luckily for Alice, the cook went on stirring the soup, paying no mind to the Duchess's instruction.

"Well, then," the Duchess continued, "don't bother me. I never was good with figures. Here," she said as she handed Alice the baby, "you hold him. I must get ready to play croquet with the Queen."

Alice took the baby outside to get some

air. "What an odd little thing," she thought. The baby held its arms and legs out in all directions like a starfish, and was snorting nonstop like a steam engine. "If I don't take this child away with me," she said, "they're sure to kill it in a day or two. It would be criminal to leave it behind."

At this, the baby let out a loud grunt. "Don't grunt," Alice scolded. "That's not a proper way to express yourself."

The baby grunted again, and Alice looked anxiously into its face to see what was wrong with it. The child had a *very* odd-looking face. Its nose was turned up and looked more like a pig's snout than a human nose, and its eyes were very small. Alice decided that she did not like the look of the thing at all.

She was beginning to think to herself, "Now, what would I do with this creature once I get home?" when it grunted again, so violently that she looked back down at its face with alarm. The baby had turned into a pig! Alice felt that it would be silly to carry the pig with her any farther. She set the creature down and was relieved to see it trot happily away into the woods. "If it had grown up as a human," Alice mused, "it would have made a dreadfully ugly child, but it makes a handsome pig."

Chapter 10

The Cheshire Cat

Alice was startled to see the Cheshire Cat sitting in a tree just ahead of her. The Cat grinned when it saw Alice, but did nothing more.

"Cheshire Cat," Alice began timidly, "would you tell me, please, which way I ought to go from here?"

"That depends a good deal on where you want to go," the Cat replied.

"I don't much care where . . ." began Alice.

"Then it doesn't matter which way you go," said the Cat.

"—so long as I get *somewhere*," Alice continued.

"Oh, you're sure to do that," said the Cat, "if you walk long enough."

"Well, that makes sense," Alice thought. "What sort of people live around here?" she asked.

"In that direction," the Cat said, waving his front right paw, "lives the Hatter. In that direction," waving his front left paw, "lives the March Hare. You could visit either one. They're both mad. Completely insane."

"But I don't want to meet any mad people," Alice remarked.

"Oh, you can't help that," the Cat replied. "We're all mad here. I'm mad. You're mad."

"How do you know *I'm* mad?" said Alice.

"You must be," the Cat replied, "or you wouldn't have come here."

Alice didn't think that proved anything, but did not dare to say so.

"Will you play croquet with the Queen today?" the Cat asked.

"I would like to very much," Alice replied, "but I haven't been invited yet."

"You'll see me there," the Cat said, and vanished into thin air.

Alice was not surprised by this; she was getting used to odd things happening all the time. Then, suddenly, the Cat reappeared.

"What became of the baby?" it said. "I'd nearly forgotten to ask."

"It turned into a pig," Alice answered.

"I thought it might," said the Cat, and vanished once again.

Alice waited for a moment, half expecting the Cheshire Cat to reappear. It didn't, so Alice began to walk toward where the March Hare was said to live. "I've seen hatters before," she thought to herself. "A March Hare will be much more interesting. Perhaps, since this is May, it won't be raving mad—at least not as mad as it is in March."

As she thought this, the Cat suddenly appeared again, sitting in another tree that stood before her.

"Did you say *pig* or *fig*?" the Cat asked.

"I said *pig*," replied Alice. "I wish you wouldn't keep appearing and disappearing so suddenly. It can make a person quite dizzy!"

"As you wish," said the Cat. It then began to vanish quite slowly, beginning with the end of its tail and ending with

its grin, which remained for some time after the rest of it had gone.

"Well," Alice said, "I've often seen a cat without a grin, but a grin without a cat? It must be the strangest thing I've seen in all my life!"

Soon Alice approached the back of a large house. It had two chimneys shaped like rabbit ears and a roof thatched with fur. "This must be the March Hare's house," she thought. The house was so big that Alice decided to

nibble on the left-hand bit of mushroom she still had in her pocket. She nibbled until she had grown a bit taller. Even then, she walked toward the house timidly, saying to herself, "Suppose the March Hare is raving mad, after all? I wish I'd gone to see the Hatter instead!"

Chapter 11

A Mad Tea Party

A table was set out under a tree in front of the rabbit-shaped house, and the March Hare and the Hatter were having tea at it. A dormouse was sitting between them, fast asleep, and the other two were using it as a cushion, resting their elbows on it and talking over its head.

"That must be uncomfortable for the Dormouse," Alice thought, "but since it's asleep, I suppose it doesn't mind."

The table was large, with many empty

places set, but the three were all crowded together at one corner. "No room! No room!" they cried out when they saw Alice coming.

"There's plenty of room," she said, annoyed, and sat down in a large arm-chair at one end.

"Have some juice," the March Hare offered.

Alice looked around the table, but saw nothing to drink but tea. "I don't see any juice," she said.

"That's because there isn't any," said the March Hare.

"Then it wasn't very polite of you to offer it," Alice replied.

"It wasn't very polite of you to sit down without being invited," the Hare snapped back.

"I didn't know that it was *your* table," said Alice. "It's been set for many more than three."

Alice noticed that the Hatter was staring at her. "Your hair needs to be cut," he said bluntly.

"You shouldn't make such personal remarks," Alice said. "It's very rude."

The Hatter opened his eyes very wide on hearing this, but all he said was, "Why is a raven like a writing desk?"

"Well," thought Alice, "we'll have some fun now! I love riddles." Aloud, she said, "I believe I can guess that."

"Do you mean that you think you can come up with the answer to it?" said the March Hare.

"Exactly so," replied Alice.

"Then you should say what you mean," said the March Hare.

"I do," Alice said. "At least, I mean what I say—and that's the same thing."

"It's not at all the same thing!" the Hatter cried. "Why, you might as well say that 'I see what I eat' is the same thing as 'I eat what I see.' "

"You might as well say," added the March Hare, "that 'I like what I get' is the same thing as 'I get what I like!' "

"You might as well say," the Dormouse chimed in, sleepily, "that 'I breathe when I sleep' is the same thing as 'I sleep when I breathe!' "

"It *is* the same thing with you," said the Hatter to the dormouse, and the conversation came to a halt. The group sat quietly for some time, while Alice tried to solve the riddle. She thought about everything she knew of ravens and writing desks, which wasn't much.

Eventually, the Hatter broke the silence. "What day of the month is it?" he asked as he took his watch out of his pocket. He was looking at it uneasily, shaking it now and again and putting it up to his ear.

"The fourth," said Alice.

"Two days wrong!" sighed the Hatter. He then dipped the watch into his cup of tea, pulled it out, and looked at it again.

"What a funny watch!" Alice remarked. "It tells the day of the month, but it doesn't tell you what o'clock it is!"

"Why should it?" muttered the Hatter. "Does *your* watch tell you the year?"

"Of course not," she replied, "but that's because it stays the same year for

such a long time, one doesn't need a watch to tell *that*."

"Which is just the case with mine," replied the Hatter.

Alice was puzzled. "Doesn't *anyone* in this place make sense?" she wondered. "I don't understand you," she said aloud to the Hatter, as politely as she could.

Ignoring Alice's comment, the Hatter said, "The Dormouse is asleep again."

The sleepy creature shook its head impatiently and said, without opening his eyes, "Of course, of course. That's just what I was going to say myself."

"Have you guessed the riddle yet?" the Hatter asked Alice.

"No, I give up," Alice replied. "What's the answer?"

"I haven't the slightest idea," said the Hatter.

"Nor I," said the March Hare.

Alice sighed wearily. "You might do something better with the time than wasting it asking riddles with no answers!" she said.

"If you knew Time as well as I do," replied the Hatter, "you wouldn't talk about wasting *it*. It's a *him*."

"I don't know what you mean," Alice said, confused.

"Of course you don't!" the Hatter snapped, tossing his head. "I'll bet you never even spoke to Time!"

"Perhaps not," Alice said cautiously. "But I beat time when I learn music."

"Ah! That explains it," said the Hatter. "He doesn't like being beaten. If you would keep on good terms with him, he would do almost anything you liked with the clock. For instance, suppose it were nine o'clock in the morning, time to begin lessons. All you would have to do is whisper a hint to Time, and the clock would go round in a twinkling! Half-past one, time for lunch!"

"Oh, I wish it was," the March Hare whispered to itself.

"That would be grand, certainly," said Alice thoughtfully, "but then I wouldn't be hungry for it yet."

"Not at first, perhaps," said the Hatter, "but you could keep it at half-past one as long as you liked."

"Is that the way *you* manage?" Alice asked.

The Hatter shook his head sadly. "Not I!" he replied. "I had a fight with Time last March—just before *he* went mad,

you know—" He pointed his teaspoon at
the March Hare. "It was at the great
concert given by the Queen of Hearts,
and I had to sing:

'Twinkle, twinkle, little bat!
How I wonder what you're at!'

You know the song, perhaps?"

"I've heard something like it," said
Alice.

"It goes on," the Hatter continued, "like this:

> *'Up above the world you fly,*
> *Like a tea tray in the sky.*
> *Twinkle, twinkle—'* "

Here the Dormouse began singing in its sleep, *"Twinkle, twinkle, twinkle, twinkle—"* It went on so long that they had to pinch it to make it stop.

"Well, I had hardly finished the first verse," said the Hatter, "when the Queen jumped up and cried, 'He's murdering the Time! Off with his head!' "

"How dreadful!" exclaimed Alice.

"Ever since then," the Hatter went on, mournfully, "he won't do a thing I ask! It's always six o'clock now."

"Is that why so many tea things are set out here?' Alice asked.

"Yes," said the Hatter with a sigh. "It's always tea time, and we have no time to wash the things between whiles."

"So you keep moving around the table?" asked Alice.

"Exactly so," said the Hatter, "as the things get used up."

"What happens when you come to the beginning again?" Alice dared to ask.

"Let's change the subject," the March Hare interrupted, yawning. "I'm getting tired of this. I vote that the young lady tell us a story!"

chapter 12

The Dormouse's Story

"I'm afraid I don't know one," Alice replied, alarmed at being put on the spot.

"Then the Dormouse shall tell us one!' the March Hare and the Hatter both cried. "Wake up, Dormouse! Wake up!" they exclaimed as they pinched it on both sides at once.

The Dormouse slowly opened its eyes. "I wasn't asleep," it said in a lazy voice. "I heard every word you were saying."

"Tell us a story!" said the March Hare.

"Yes, please do!" cried Alice.

"Be quick about it," said the Hatter, "or you'll be asleep again before it's done."

"Once upon a time there were three little sisters," the Dormouse began in a great hurry, "and their names were Elsie, Lacie, and Tillie; they lived at the bottom of a well—"

"What did they live on?" asked Alice, who was always interested in eating and drinking.

"On molasses," the Dormouse replied, after thinking for a moment.

"That's all?" Alice asked. "They couldn't have done that. They would have been ill!"

"So they were," said the Dormouse. "They were *very* ill."

Alice tried to imagine living that way, but it puzzled her too much. "Why did they live at the bottom of a well?"

"Take some more tea," the March Hare said to Alice.

"I haven't had any yet," Alice replied in an offended tone, "so I can't take more."

"You mean you can't take *less*," the Hatter replied. "It's very easy to take *more* than nothing."

"Nobody asked *your* opinion," Alice told him.

"Who is making personal remarks now?" the Hatter asked triumphantly.

Alice didn't know what to say to this,

so she didn't reply. Instead, she helped herself to some tea and some bread and butter, then turned to the Dormouse and repeated her question. "Why did the sisters live at the bottom of a well?"

After thinking for a moment, the Dormouse replied, "It was a molasses well."

"There is no such thing!" Alice exclaimed. She was getting very annoyed by all of this nonsense.

"If you can't be polite," the Dormouse told her, "finish the story yourself."

"No, please go on!" Alice said humbly. "I won't interrupt again."

The Dormouse sighed, then went on. "So these three little sisters, they were learning to draw, you know—"

"What did they draw?" asked Alice, interrupting again.

"Molasses," said the Dormouse, without thinking at all this time.

"I want a clean cup," interrupted the Hatter. "Let's all move one place over."

He moved on as he spoke, and the Dormouse followed him. The March Hare moved into the Dormouse's place, and Alice took the place of the March Hare. The Hatter was the only one who got any advantage from the change. Alice was worse off than before, because the March Hare had spilled milk onto his plate.

Alice didn't wish to offend the Dormouse again, so she asked cautiously, "I don't understand. Where did they draw the molasses *from*?"

"You can draw water out of a water well," said the Hatter, "so I should think you could draw molasses out of a molasses well."

"But they were *in* the well," Alice said to the Dormouse.

"Of course they were," said the Dormouse, "well in the well."

Poor Alice was so confused by now that she let the Dormouse go on.

"They were learning to draw," the Dormouse went on, yawning and rubbing its eyes, for it was getting sleepy. "They drew all sorts of things—everything that begins with an *M*—"

"Why with an *M*?" said Alice.

"Why not?" said the March Hare.

Alice was silent. There seemed to be no use in asking questions.

The Dormouse was beginning to doze

off, so the Hatter pinched it. The creature woke again with a little shriek and went on. "Everything that begins with an *M*, such as mousetraps, and the moon, and memory, and muchness—did you ever see such a thing as a drawing of a muchness?"

"Well, now that you ask me," said Alice, very much confused, "I don't think—"

"Then you shouldn't talk," said the Hatter, smirking.

This rudeness was more than Alice could take. She got up in disgust and walked off. The Dormouse fell asleep instantly, and neither of the others paid any attention to Alice's leaving. She looked back once or twice, half-hoping that they would call her back. The last she saw of them, they were trying to stuff the sleepy Dormouse into the teapot.

"I'll never go *there* again!" said Alice, as she walked through the woods. "It's the stupidest tea party I ever was at in all my life!"

Just as she said this, Alice noticed that one of the trees in front of her had a door leading into it. "That's curious!" she thought. "But everything is curious today. I may as well go in." And in she went.

Alice found herself back in the long hall with the little glass table. "I'll manage better this time," she said to herself. She began by taking the little golden key and unlocking the door that led into the beautiful garden. Then she nibbled at

the mushroom—she still had pieces of it in her pocket—until she was about a foot high. She went through the door, then down a little passage, and found herself at last in the beautiful garden among bright flower beds and cool fountains.

chapter 13

The Queen's Garden

A large rose tree stood near the entrance to the garden. The roses growing on it were white, but three gardeners were busily painting them red. Alice thought this a very curious thing, and went nearer to watch them. Even more curious was the fact that these gardeners were not people, but playing cards with heads, arms, and legs sticking out of their card bodies. As she approached, one said, "Look out, Five! Don't go splashing paint on me like that!"

"I couldn't help it," said Five, in a sulky tone. "Seven bumped my elbow."

At that, Seven looked up and said, "That's right, Five! Always blame others!"

"*You'd* better not talk!" responded Five. "I heard the Queen say only yesterday that you deserved to be beheaded!"

"What for?" asked the gardener who had spoken first.

"That's none of *your* business, Two!" said Seven.

"Yes, it *is* his business," said Five, "and I'll tell him why! It was for giving the cook tulip roots instead of onions."

Seven threw down his brush, and was yelling, "Well, of all the unfair things!" when he noticed Alice and stopped himself suddenly. The others looked around then, too, and all of them bowed low.

"Would you tell me, please," said Alice timidly, "why you are painting those white roses red?"

Five and Seven were silent, and looked at Two. Two began, in a low voice, "Well, you see, Miss, this ought to have been a *red* rose tree, but we planted a white one by mistake. If the Queen finds out, she'll have our heads cut off. So we're doing our best, before she comes, to hide—"

At this moment Five, who had been anxiously looking across the garden, called out, "The Queen! The Queen!" The three gardeners threw themselves flat on

their faces. There was a sound of many footsteps, and Alice looked around, eager to see this queen she had been hearing so much about.

First came 10 soldiers carrying clubs. Like the three gardeners, they were playing cards. Next came 10 courtiers, and they were cards as well. These were ornamented all over with diamonds. After these came the 10 royal children, jumping merrily along, hand in hand. They were all ornamented with hearts.

Next came the guests, mostly kings and queens. Among them, Alice recognized the White Rabbit. It was talking in a hurried, nervous manner, smiling at everything that was said. It passed Alice without noticing her.

The Knave of Hearts then followed, carrying the King's crown on a crimson velvet cushion. Then, last of all in this grand procession, came the King and the Queen of Hearts.

Alice didn't know whether she ought to lie down on her face as the three gardeners had, but she couldn't remember ever having heard of such a rule. "Besides," she thought, "what would be the use of a procession if people had to lie down on their faces and not be able to see it?" She decided to stand where she was and watch.

The procession marched forward, eventually arriving opposite Alice. They

thought, "They're only a pack of cards! I need not be afraid of them."

"Who are *these* three?" said the Queen, pointing to the gardeners lying next to the rose tree.

"How should *I* know?" said Alice, surprised at her own courage. "It's no business of *mine.*"

The Queen turned red with fury and, after glaring at Alice like a wild beast, began screaming, "Off with her head! Off with her—"

"Nonsense!" said Alice very loudly and decidedly, and the Queen was silent.

The King laid his hand on the Queen's arm and timidly said, "Consider this, my dear, she is only a child!"

The Queen turned angrily away from him and glared at the three gardeners lying on the ground. "Turn them over!" she said to the Knave.

The Knave did so, very carefully, with one foot.

"Get up!" cried the Queen, in a shrill

all stopped and looked at her,
Queen said severely, "Who is this
said it to the Knave of Hearts, whe
bowed and smiled in reply.

"You don't know a thing," said
Queen, tossing her head impatient.
She turned to Alice and asked, "What
your name, child?"

"My name is Alice, Your Majesty," said
Alice very politely, but to herself she

voice. The gardeners jumped up and began bowing to the King, the Queen, the royal children, and everybody else.

"Stop that!" screamed the Queen. "You're making me dizzy." Turning to the rose tree, she went on. "What *have* you been doing here?"

"May it please, Your Majesty," said Two, very humbly, bending down on one knee, "we were only trying to—"

"*I* see!" said the Queen, who had been carefully examining the roses. "Off with their heads!"

The procession moved on, with three of the soldiers remaining behind to execute the unfortunate gardeners, who ran to Alice for protection.

"You won't be beheaded!" Alice told the gardeners in an encouraging tone. While no one was looking, she spied a large flowerpot that stood nearby where they could hide. The three soldiers wandered about for a while, looking for them, then quietly marched off after the others.

"Are their heads off?" shouted the Queen.

"Their heads are gone, Your Majesty!" the soldiers replied.

"Good!" shouted the Queen. "You," she called to Alice. "Can you play croquet?"

"Yes!" Alice replied with enthusiasm.

"Come on, then!" roared the Queen. So Alice joined the procession, wondering what would happen next.

Chapter 14

A Game of Croquet

As Alice walked, she heard a timid voice at her side saying, "It's—it's a very fine day!" Alice looked down to see that she was walking next to the White Rabbit, who was peering anxiously into her face.

"Yes, very," Alice agreed. "Where is the Duchess?"

"Hush! Hush!" said the White Rabbit in a low, hurried tone, looking anxiously over his shoulder. He raised himself up on tiptoe, put his mouth close to her ear, and whispered, "She's under sentence of execution."

"What for?" said Alice.

"Did you say, 'What a pity'?" the White Rabbit asked.

"No, I didn't," said Alice. "I said, 'What for?' "

"She boxed the Queen's ears," the Rabbit began, and Alice laughed loudly. "Oh, hush!" the Rabbit whispered in a frightened tone. "The Queen will hear you! You see, the Duchess arrived rather late, and the Queen said—"

The Rabbit was interrupted by the Queen, who thundered, "Get to your places at once!" People began running in all directions, tumbling against each other. After a minute or two, they got settled and the game began.

Alice had never seen such a curious croquet field in her life. The balls were live hedgehogs and the mallets were live flamingoes. To make the arches, the card soldiers doubled themselves over and stood on their hands and feet. Alice had never seen anything like it before and wondered if she would be able to play at all.

Alice's first problem was managing her flamingo mallet. She got its body tucked away comfortably enough under her arm, with its legs hanging down, but then ran into trouble. Just when she got its neck straightened out and was about to tap the hedgehog ball with the flamingo-mallet's head, the flamingo would twist itself around and look up at her face. It had such a puzzled expression that Alice burst out laughing.

When she finally got the flamingo's head down and was ready to begin, the hedgehog ball unrolled itself and crawled away. "This is a very difficult game indeed!" cried Alice, quite frustrated.

The other players played all at once, without waiting for turns. They argued the whole time and fought over the hedgehogs. The Queen was soon in a furious fit and went stamping across the field, shouting, "Off with his head!" or "Off with her head!" about once a minute. The entire croquet field was in chaos.

Alice began to feel very uneasy. She had not had any dispute with the Queen, but that could happen any minute. "What would become of me then?" she wondered. "They're awfully fond of beheading people here. It's amazing that there is anyone left alive!"

Alice was looking around for some way of escape and wondering how to get

away without being seen when she noticed a curious object floating in the air. It puzzled her very much at first, but after watching it a minute or two, she realized that it was a grin. "It's the Cheshire Cat!" she thought happily. "Now I shall have somebody to talk to."

"How are you getting on?" said the Cat, as soon as it had enough mouth to speak with.

Alice waited until the Cat's eyes appeared, then nodded. "There's no use speaking to it," she thought, "until at least one of its ears has come back."

In another minute, the whole head had appeared. Alice put down her flamingo-mallet and began to tell the Cat about the game, feeling very glad to have someone to listen to her. The Cat seemed to think that enough of its body was now in sight—no more of it appeared.

"They don't play at all fairly," Alice said. "They argue so much that one can't hear oneself speak. They don't seem to have any rules in particular. If they do, nobody pays attention to them! You have no idea how confusing it is with all the game parts being alive! For instance, the arch I'm supposed to go through next is over there, wandering about at the other end of the field! And I should have croqueted the Queen's hedgehog, but it ran away when it saw mine coming!"

"How do you like the Queen?" asked the Cat in a low voice.

"Not at all," said Alice honestly. "She's so very—" Just then, she noticed that the Queen was close behind her, listening, so she went on, "—so very likely to win that it's hardly worthwhile finishing the game."

The Queen smiled and walked on.

The King, who had been right behind her, stopped to talk to Alice. "Who are you talking to?" he asked, looking at the Cat's head with great curiosity.

"It's a friend of mine, a Cheshire Cat," said Alice. "Allow me to introduce it."

"I don't like the look of it at all," said the King. "However, it may kiss my hand if it likes."

"I'd rather not," the Cat remarked.

"Don't be rude," said the King, "and don't look at me like that." He got behind Alice as he spoke.

"A cat may look at a king," Alice said.

"I've read that in some book, but I don't remember where."

"Well, it must be removed," said the King very decidedly, and he called to the Queen, who was passing at the moment, "My dear! I wish you would have this cat removed!"

The Queen had only one way of settling all difficulties, be they big or small. "Off with its head!" she said, without even looking round.

"I'll fetch the executioner myself," said the King eagerly, and he hurried off.

Alice decided to go see how the game was progressing. She heard the Queen's voice in the distance, screaming loudly as usual. The Queen had already sentenced three players to be executed for having missed their turns. That worried Alice. The game was in such confusion, she couldn't tell whether it was her turn or not. So she went looking for her hedgehog.

She found it fighting with another

hedgehog. This seemed like a great chance to hit one of them into the other. Her flamingo-mallet, however, was on the other side of the garden, trying to fly up into a tree. By the time Alice had caught it and brought it back, the fight was over and both hedgehogs had disappeared. "It doesn't matter much," thought Alice, "since all the arches have left this side of the field." She tucked her flamingo-mallet under her arm so it would not escape again, and went back for a little more conversation with her friend, the Cheshire Cat.

When Alice got back to the Cat, she was surprised to find a large crowd around it. Some sort of dispute was going on among the executioner, the King, and the Queen. The moment they saw Alice, all three demanded that she settle the question, and repeated their arguments to her. They all spoke at once, making it very hard to understand what they said.

The executioner's argument was that you couldn't cut off a head unless there was a body to cut it off from. He had never done such a thing before, and he wasn't going to begin at this point.

The King's argument was that anything that had a head could be beheaded.

The Queen's argument was that if something wasn't done about it in less than no time, she would have everybody executed. (This last remark was making everyone look very anxious.)

"Why don't you ask the Duchess?" Alice suggested. "It's *her* cat."

"She's in prison," the Queen said to the executioner. "Bring her here." The executioner went off like an arrow.

The Cat's head began fading away the moment the executioner was gone. By the time he had returned with the Duchess, the Cat had disappeared entirely. The King and the executioner ran wildly up and down looking for it. The rest of the party went back to the game.

Chapter 15

Reunion With the Duchess

"You can't imagine how glad I am to see you again, you dear old thing!" said the Duchess, tucking her arm affectionately into Alice's as they walked off together.

Alice was glad to find the Duchess in such a good mood. Perhaps it was only the pepper that had made her so mean earlier. "When *I'm* a Duchess," Alice thought, "I won't have any pepper in my

kitchen *at all.* Soup does very well without pepper. Maybe it's always pepper that makes people hot-tempered," she went on, pleased at having found a new kind of rule. "Vinegar, that makes people sour, and sugar makes children sweet-tempered. I wish people knew *that*! If they did, they wouldn't be so stingy about candy and cakes."

Lost in her thoughts, Alice had forgotten about the Duchess, and so was startled to hear a voice close to her ear. "You're thinking about something, my dear," said the Duchess, "and that makes you forget to talk. I can't tell you what the moral of that is, but I'll remember it soon."

"Perhaps it doesn't have a moral," Alice remarked.

"Tsk, tsk, child!" the Duchess scolded. "Everything has a moral, if only you can find it." She squeezed herself closer to Alice's side as she spoke.

"The game is getting on better now,"

Alice said, trying to keep up the conversation.

"Yes," said the Duchess, "and the moral of that is, 'Oh, 'tis love, 'tis love, that makes the world go round.'"

"I believe you once said," Alice whispered, "that it's done by everybody minding their own business!"

The Duchess rested her sharp little

chin on Alice's shoulder, which Alice didn't like much. "Ah, well! It means almost the same thing," said the Duchess, "and the moral of *that* is: 'Take care of the sense, and the sounds will take care of themselves.'"

"How fond she is of finding morals in things!" Alice thought to herself, "But they make no sense at all!"

"I'm not sure what your flamingo thinks of me being so close," the Duchess said after a pause.

"He might bite," Alice cautioned, hoping the Duchess would go away.

"Very true," said the Duchess. "Flamingoes and mustard both bite, and the moral of that is, 'Birds of a feather flock together.'"

"Mustard is not a bird," said Alice, pointing out the obvious.

"Right, as usual," said the Duchess. "What a clear way you have of putting things!" Suddenly, her smile faded and Alice felt her begin to tremble. Alice looked up. There stood the Queen in front of them, with her arms folded, frowning like a thunderstorm.

"A fine day, Your Majesty!" said the Duchess in a timid voice.

"I give you fair warning," shouted the Queen, stamping on the ground. "Either you or your head must be off, in about half, or no, time! Take your choice!"

The Duchess took her choice, and was gone in a moment.

"Let's go on with the game," the Queen said to Alice. Too frightened to say a word, poor Alice slowly followed the Queen back to the croquet field.

The other guests had taken advantage of the Queen's absence by resting in the shade. The moment they saw her, however, they hurried back to the game. The Queen remarked that a moment's delay would cost them their lives. So the game went on.

All the time they were playing, the Queen argued with the other players.

"Off with his head!" or "Off with her head!" was heard throughout the competition. Anyone the Queen sentenced was taken into custody by the soldiers, who had to stop being arches to do so. After half an hour or so, there were no arches left and all the players—all except the King, the Queen, and Alice—were in custody and under sentence of execution.

chapter 16

The Mock Turtle

The Queen, quite out of breath, then walked over to Alice and said, "Have you seen the Mock Turtle yet?"

"No," said Alice. "I don't even know what a mock turtle is."

"It's the thing that mock turtle soup is made from," said the Queen.

"I never saw one or heard of one," said Alice.

"Come on, then," said the Queen. "He shall tell you his history."

As they walked off together, Alice heard the King say in a low voice to the gathered company, "You are all pardoned."

"Well, that's a relief!" Alice said to herself, for she had been unhappy about the number of executions the Queen had ordered.

She and the Queen soon came upon an odd-looking beast that looked very much like a dragon. It was lying fast asleep in the sun. "That's a gryphon," said the Queen to Alice, who looked curiously at the creature.

"Up, you lazy thing!" said the Queen. "Take this young lady to see the Mock Turtle and hear his story. I must go

back and see to some executions I've ordered." She walked off, leaving Alice alone with the Gryphon.

Alice did not like the look of the creature, but thought it would be as safe to stay with the Gryphon as it would be to stay with that savage Queen.

The Gryphon sat up and rubbed its eyes. It watched the Queen until she was out of sight, then chuckled. "What fun!" it said to Alice, with a devilish grin.

"What *is* the fun?" Alice asked.

"*She* is," the Gryphon replied. "The Queen. It's all her imagination, you know, ordering people's heads off. They never really execute anyone. Come on!"

"Everybody says 'Come on!' here," thought Alice, as she walked after the creature. "I've never been so ordered about in all my life!"

They had not gone far before they saw the Mock Turtle, who looked extremely odd. He had the head and tail of a cow and the back legs of a goat. He also had a shell and flippers, like a turtle. He was, indeed, an odd sight.

He was sitting sad and lonely on a little ledge of rock. As they came nearer, Alice could hear him sighing as if his heart would break. She pitied him deeply. "What is his sorrow?" she asked the Gryphon.

"He hasn't any sorrow," was the reply. "It's all in his imagination, you know."

They went up to the Mock Turtle, who looked at them silently with large eyes full of tears.

"This young lady here," said the Gryphon, "wants to hear your story."

"I'll tell it to her," the Mock Turtle replied in a deep, hollow tone. "Sit down, both of you, and don't speak a word till I've finished."

They both did as they were told, and the three sat in silence for some time. "I don't see how he can ever finish, if he doesn't begin," Alice thought.

At last, the Mock Turtle began. "Once," he said, with a deep sigh, "I was a real turtle. When we were little we went to school in the sea. The master was an old turtle; we used to call him 'Tortoise'."

"Why did you call him 'Tortoise'," Alice asked, "if he wasn't one?"

"We called him *Tortoise* because he *taught us*," said the Mock Turtle angrily. "Really, you are very dim!"

"You ought to be ashamed of yourself for asking such a simple question," added the Gryphon. Then both creatures sat silently and looked at poor

Alice for such a long time, that she felt ready to sink into the earth.

At last the Gryphon said to the Mock Turtle, "Drive on, old fellow! Don't be all day about it!"

"All right," he continued. "We went to school in the sea, though you may not believe it."

"I never said I didn't!" cried Alice.

"You did," said the Mock Turtle.

"Hold your tongue!" added the Gryphon, before Alice could speak again. The Mock Turtle went on.

"We had the best education. In fact, we went to school every day."

"So do I," said Alice. "You needn't be so proud of that."

"With extra courses?" asked the Mock Turtle.

"Yes," said Alice, "French and music."

"And washing?" asked the Mock Turtle.

"Certainly not!" said Alice.

"Ah! Then yours isn't a really good

school," said the Mock Turtle in a tone of great relief. "Now at *ours*, they had French, music, *and* washing."

"I don't see what use washing would be," Alice said, "since you lived at the bottom of the ocean."

"It was very helpful, indeed. We also learned Reeling, Writhing, and Arithmetic, including Uglification."

"Uglification!" exclaimed Alice. "What's that?"

The Gryphon lifted its paws in surprise. "What? Never heard of uglifying! You know what to beautify is, I suppose?"

"Yes," said Alice doubtfully. "It means to make something prettier."

"Well, then," said the Gryphon, "if you don't know what to uglify is, you *are* dim."

Tired of the insults, Alice decided to ignore the Gryphon. Instead, she turned back to the Mock Turtle. "What else did you learn?" she asked

"Well, there was Mystery," the Mock Turtle replied, counting off the subjects on his flappers. "Mystery, both ancient and modern. And Seaography. Then Drawling—the Drawling master was an old eel that used to come once a week. He taught us Drawling, Stretching, and Fainting in Coils."

Alice had heard of drawing, sketching, and painting in oils, but obviously these were something different. Her head was spinning with confusion, but she went along with the Mock Turtle's story just the same. "How many hours a day did you do these lessons?" she asked.

"Ten hours the first day," said the Mock Turtle, "nine the next, and so on."

"What a curious plan!" said Alice.

"That's why they're called *lessons*," said the Gryphon, "because they *lessen* from day to day."

This was a new idea to Alice. She thought it over for a moment, then said, "Then the eleventh day must have been a holiday?"

"Of course it was," said the Mock Turtle. "Perhaps you're not so dim, after all."

Alice was about to ask what happened on the twelfth day, when a loud cry was heard from the distance.

"The trial is beginning!" shouted a far-away voice.

"Come on!" cried the Gryphon. It grabbed Alice by the hand and they hurried off, leaving the Mock Turtle behind.

"What trial?" Alice panted as she ran, but the Gryphon only said, "Come on!' and ran faster, pulling Alice along so swiftly that her feet barely touched the ground.

Chapter 17

Who Stole the Tarts?

When the Gryphon and Alice arrived, they found the King and Queen of Hearts seated on their thrones. A big crowd was gathered about them—all sorts of little birds and beasts, as well as the whole pack of cards. The Knave was standing before them, in chains, with a soldier on each side to guard him.

Near the King was the White Rabbit, with a trumpet in one hand and a scroll of parchment in the other. In the middle of the court was a table with a large dish of tarts on it. They looked so good, it made Alice hungry. "I wish they would finish the trial quickly," she thought, "and start handing out the refreshments!" There seemed to be no chance of this, though, so she looked at everything about her, to pass the time.

Alice had never been in a court of justice before, but she had read about them in books and was pleased to find that she knew the name of nearly everything there. "That's the judge," she said to herself, "wearing that big white wig." Alice noticed that the judge was also the King.

"That's the jury box," thought Alice, "and those twelve creatures must be the jurors." She said this last word two or three times to herself, being rather proud of knowing it. She recognized that one of the jurors was Bill the Lizard.

The 12 jurors were all writing busily with chalk on little slates.

"What are they doing?' Alice whispered

to the Gryphon. "They can't have anything to write yet, because the trial has
not begun!"

"They're putting down their names," the
Gryphon whispered in reply, "in case they
forget them before the end of the trial."

"Stupid things!" Alice began in a loud, indignant voice, just as the White Rabbit cried out, "Silence in the court!"

Alice could see that all the jurors were writing "Stupid things!" on their slates. One of them didn't know how to spell *stupid* and had to ask his neighbor.

"Herald, read the accusation!" ordered the King.

At this the White Rabbit blew three blasts on the trumpet, then unrolled the parchment scroll and read as follows:

> *"The Queen of Hearts, she*
> *made some tarts,*
> *All on a summer day:*
> *The Knave of Hearts, he*
> *stole those tarts,*
> *And took them quite away!"*

chapter 18
The Hatter and the Cook Testify

"Call the first witness," said the King.

The Rabbit blew three blasts on the trumpet and called out, "First witness!"

The first witness was the Mad Hatter. He came in with a teacup in one hand and a piece of bread and butter in the other. "I beg your pardon, Your Majesty," he said, "for bringing these in, but I hadn't finished my tea when I was sent for."

"You ought to have finished," said the King. "When did you begin?"

The Hatter looked at the March Hare, who had followed him into the court, arm in arm with the Dormouse. "Fourteenth of March, I think it was," he said.

"Fifteenth," said the March Hare.

"Sixteenth," said the Dormouse.

"Write that down," the King told the jury, and the jurors eagerly wrote all three dates on their slates.

"Take off your hat," the King told the Hatter.

"It isn't mine," the Hatter replied.

"Stolen!" the King exclaimed, turning to the jurors, who immediately made note of the fact.

"Oh, no! I keep them to sell," the Hatter explained. "I have none of my own. I'm a hatter, you see."

Here the Queen put on her spectacles and began staring at the Hatter, who turned pale and fidgeted.

"Give your evidence," said the King, "and don't be nervous or I'll have you executed on the spot."

This did not encourage the witness at all. He kept shifting from one foot to the other and looking uneasily at the Queen. In his confusion, he bit a large piece out of his teacup instead of his bread and butter.

At this moment, Alice felt an odd sensation, which puzzled her until she realized what it was. She was beginning to grow larger again! At first she thought she would get up and leave, but decided to stay as long as there was room for her.

"I wish you wouldn't squeeze so," said

the Dormouse, who was sitting next to her. "I can hardly breathe."

"I can't help it," Alice said quietly. "I'm growing."

"Well, you have no right to grow *here*," the Dormouse replied lazily.

"Don't talk nonsense," said Alice. "You're growing, too."

"Yes, but I grow at a normal pace," said the Dormouse, "not in that ridiculous fashion." With that, it got up and crossed to the other side of the court.

"Give your evidence," the King repeated angrily, "or I'll have you executed, whether you're nervous or not."

"I'm a poor man, Your Majesty," the Mad Hatter began, his voice trembling. "I hadn't begun my tea, and with the bread and butter getting so thin, and the twinkling of the tea—"

"The twinkling of the *what*?" asked the King, confused.

"It began with the tea," the Hatter replied.

"Of course *twinkling* begins with a *T*!" the King snapped. "Do you take me for an idiot? Go on!"

"I'm a poor man," the Hatter went on, "and most things twinkled after that, only the March Hare said—"

"I did not!" the March Hare interrupted.

"You did!" said the Hatter.

"Did not!" said the March Hare.

"He says that he didn't," said the King to the jury. "Leave out that part."

"Well, at any rate," the Hatter continued, "the Dormouse said—" and the Hatter trailed off for a moment. He looked anxiously around the room to see if the Dormouse would argue, too, but it was fast asleep. "After that," the Hatter went on, "I cut some more bread and butter."

"But what did the Dormouse say?" one juror asked.

"I can't remember," said the Hatter.

"You *must* remember,' remarked the King, "or I'll have you executed."

The terrified Hatter dropped his teacup and bread and butter, and got down on one knee. "I'm a poor man, Your Majesty—" he began.

"You're a very poor *speaker*," said the King, "but if that's all you know about it, you may step down."

Relieved, the Hatter hurriedly left the court, leaving his teacup and bread and butter behind.

"Take off his head outside," said the Queen to one of the officers, but the Hatter was out of sight before the officer could reach the door.

"Call the next witness!" said the King.

Alice guessed who the next witness was before she appeared by the way the people near the door began sneezing all at once. It was the Duchess's cook, carrying the pepper box in her hand.

"Give your evidence," said the King.

"I won't," said the cook.

The King looked anxiously at the White Rabbit, who said in a low voice,

"Your Majesty must cross-examine *this* witness."

"Well, if I must, I must," the King said and, after folding his arms and frowning at the cook until his eyes were nearly out of sight, he said in a deep voice, "What are tarts made of?"

"Pepper, mostly," answered the cook.

"Molasses," said a sleepy voice behind her.

"Grab that Dormouse," shrieked the Queen. "Behead that Dormouse! Turn that Dormouse out of court! Pinch him! Off with his whiskers!"

For some minutes the whole court was in confusion while the Dormouse was put out. By the time they had settled down again, the cook had disappeared.

"Never mind! Call the next witness," said the King, sounding relieved. "My dear," he muttered to the Queen, "why don't *you* cross-examine the next witness? It makes my head ache!"

Alice watched the White Rabbit fumble over the list and wondered what the next witness would be like. "They don't have much evidence yet," she said to herself. Imagine her surprise when the White Rabbit read out, at the top of his shrill little voice, the name "Alice."

Chapter 19
Alice's Evidence

"Here!" cried Alice, forgetting in her excitement how large she had grown in the last few minutes. She jumped up so fast that she knocked over the jury box with the edge of her skirt, spilling the jurors onto the heads of the crowd below.

"Oh, I *beg* your pardon!" she cried, picking them up as quickly as she could.

"The trial cannot proceed," said the King in a grave voice, "until all the jurors

are back in their proper places. *All* of them," he repeated, looking hard at Alice.

Alice noticed that, in her haste, she had put Bill the Lizard in upside down. The poor little thing was waving its tail about, unable to move. She plucked it out and put it back in the box, right side up.

As soon as the jurors had recovered from the shock of their fall, and their slates and chalk had been found and handed back to them, they set to work writing out a history of the accident. All, that is, except Bill the Lizard, who seemed too stunned to do anything but sit with his mouth open, gazing at the courtroom roof.

"What do you know about this business?" the King said to Alice.

"Nothing," said Alice.

"Nothing *whatsoever*?" said the King.

"Nothing whatever," said Alice.

"That's very important," the King said, turning to the jurors.

They were beginning to write this on

their slates when the White Rabbit interrupted. "*Un*important, Your Majesty means, of course," he said.

"Of course—*un*important, I meant," said the King, then went on to himself, "important—unimportant—unimportant—important," as if he were trying to decide which word sounded best.

Alice noticed that some of the jurors wrote *important* and some wrote *unimportant*. "It doesn't matter, either way," she thought.

At this moment the King, who had been busily writing in his notebook, called out, "Silence!" and read from his book. "Rule Forty-two: *All persons more than a mile high must leave the court.*"

Everybody looked at Alice.

"*I'm* not a mile high," she said.

"You are," said the King.

"Nearly two miles high," said the Queen.

"Well, I won't go," said Alice. "Besides, that's not a regular rule. You invented it just now!"

"It's the oldest rule in the book," said the King.

"Then it ought to be Number One," said Alice, "not Forty-two."

The King turned pale and shut his notebook. "What is your verdict?" he asked the jury, in a low, trembling voice.

"There's more evidence to come, Your Majesty," said the White Rabbit, jumping up in a great hurry. "This paper has just arrived."

"What's in it?" asked the Queen.

"It seems to be a letter," the Rabbit replied, "written by the prisoner—the Knave—to somebody."

"Of course it was," said the King, "unless it was written to *nobody*, which isn't usual."

"*Nothing* is usual here," thought Alice.

"Who is it addressed to?" asked one of the jurors.

"It isn't addressed at all," said the White Rabbit. "There's nothing written on the outside." He unfolded the paper, then said, "It isn't a letter, after all. It's a set of verses."

"Are they in the prisoner's handwriting?" asked another juror.

"No," said the White Rabbit, "and that's the oddest thing about it." The jurors looked puzzled.

"He must have copied someone else's handwriting," said the King.

"Please, Your Majesty," said the Knave, who had remained silent until this point. "I didn't write it and they can't prove I did! There's no name signed at the end."

"If you didn't sign it," said the King, "that only makes the matter worse. You *must* have been up to no good or you would have signed your name like an honest man."

The court burst into applause at this comment; it was the first clever thing the King had said all day.

"That *proves* his guilt, of course," said the Queen.

"It proves no such thing!" said Alice. "You don't even know what the verses are about!"

"That's true," said the King, and turned to the Rabbit. "Read them."

The White Rabbit put on his spectacles. "Where shall I begin, Your Majesty?" he asked.

"Begin at the beginning," the King said gravely, "and go on until you come to the end. Then stop."

So the Rabbit read:

"They told me you had been to her,
And mentioned me to him.
She gave me a good character,
But said I could not swim.

He sent them word I had not gone
(We know it to be true):
If she should push the matter on,
What would become of you?

I gave her one, they gave him two,
You gave us three or more;
They all returned from him to you,
Though they were mine before.

My idea was that you had been
(Before she had this fit)
An obstacle that came between
Him, and ourselves, and it.

Don't let him know she liked them best,
For this must ever be
A secret, kept from all the rest,
Between yourself and me."

"That is the most important piece of evidence we have heard yet," said the King, rubbing his hands.

"Nonsense!" said Alice. "If anyone can explain it, I'll give him sixpence. *I* don't believe it means anything at all!" She had grown so large in the last few minutes that she wasn't a bit afraid of interrupting.

The jurors all wrote on their slates, "*She* doesn't believe it means anything at all," but none of them seemed to understand what was going on.

"If it doesn't mean anything," said the King, "that saves us a lot of trouble, because then we don't have to figure it out. Yet," he went on, spreading out the odd verses on his knee and looking at them with one eye, "I seem to see some meaning in this, after all. '*Said I could not swim.*' You can't swim, can you?" he asked the Knave.

The Knave shook his head sadly. "Do I look like I can swim?" he said. As he was made of cardboard, the answer was clearly no.

"All right, so far," said the King. "Now, '*We know it to be true.*' That's the jury, of course. '*I gave her one, they gave him two*'; that must be what he did with the tarts."

"But look at the rest," said Alice. "It says, '*They all returned from him to you.*'"

"And there they are!" said the King triumphantly, pointing to the tarts on the table. "Nothing can be clearer than *that*. Now, '*Before she had this fit—*' You've never had a fit, have you, my dear?" he asked the Queen.

"Never!" said the Queen furiously, throwing an inkstand at Bill the Lizard as she spoke.

"Then these words don't *fit* you," said
the King, looking round the court with a
smile. There was a dead silence.

"It's a pun! I just made a joke!" said
the King, sounding offended, so everybody laughed. "Let the jury consider its
verdict," he went on.

"No, no!" said the Queen. "Sentence
first, verdict afterward."

"That's ridiculous!" said Alice, quite loudly. "You can't have the sentence first—how unfair!"

"Hold your tongue!" said the Queen, turning purple.

"I won't!" Alice retorted.

"Off with her head!" the Queen shouted at the top of her voice. Nobody moved.

Alice, who had grown to her full size by this time, towered over everyone in the room. "Who's afraid of *you*?" she said. "You're nothing but a pack of cards!"

At this, the whole pack rose up into the air and came flying down upon her. Alice gave a little scream, half of fright and half of anger, and tried to beat them off. Suddenly, she found herself lying on the riverbank, with her head in the lap of her sister, who was gently brushing away some dead leaves that had fluttered from the trees onto Alice's face.

"Wake up, Alice!" said her sister. "What a long sleep you've had!"

"Oh, my!" said Alice. "I've had such a

curious dream!" She told her sister, as well as she could remember, all the strange adventures that you have just been reading about. When she had finished, her sister gave her a kiss and said, "It *was* a curious dream, dear, but now run on in to your tea. It's getting late." So Alice got up and ran off, thinking, as she ran, what a wonderful dream it had been.

The End

ABOUT THE AUTHOR

Lewis Carroll was born Charles Lutwidge Dodgson in Daresbury, Cheshire, England, on January 27, 1832. He was the third child and oldest boy in a family of seven girls and four boys.

Dodgson had a quick and clever mind. An excellent student, he later became a lecturer in mathematics and wrote a number of books on math and logic. He also was a skilled photographer.

Dodgson loved children. He turned his talent for entertaining his sisters and brothers as a youngster toward writing stories to amuse the children of his friends and neighbors. Using the pen name Lewis Carroll, he published *Alice's Adventures in Wonderland* in 1864 and another Alice book, *Through the Looking Glass*, in 1871. Although he wrote several other children's books, it was his books about Alice that won him worldwide, lasting fame.

Dodgson died on January 14, 1898.

Treasury of Illustrated Classics™

Adventures of Huckleberry Finn
The Adventures of Pinocchio
The Adventures of Robin Hood
The Adventures of Sherlock Holmes
The Adventures of Tom Sawyer
Alice in Wonderland
Anne of Green Gables
Beauty and the Beast
Black Beauty
The Call of the Wild
Frankenstein
Great Expectations
Gulliver's Travels
Heidi
Jane Eyre
Journey to the Center of the Earth
The Jungle Book
King Arthur and the Knights of the Round Table
The Legend of Sleepy Hollow & Rip Van Winkle
A Little Princess
Little Women
Moby Dick
Oliver Twist
Peter Pan
The Prince and the Pauper
Pygmalion
Rebecca of Sunnybrook Farm
Robinson Crusoe
The Secret Garden
Swiss Family Robinson
The Time Machine
Treasure Island
20,000 Leagues Under the Sea
White Fang
The Wind in the Willows
The Wizard of Oz